h₂O

Just add water!

Living with Secrets

Adapted by Rachel Elliot

SIMON AND SCHUSTER

SIMON AND SCHUSTER
First published in Great Britain in 2009 by Simon & Schuster UK Ltd,
1st Floor, 222 Gray's Inn Road, London WC1X 8HB
A CBS Company

Originally published in Australia in 2007 by Parragon

Licenced by ZDF Enterprises GmbH, Mainz © A JMSP Programme in association with FFC,
PFTC, Network 10, ZDF German Television Network and ZDF Enterprises GmbH
© 2009 Viacom International Inc. All Rights Reserved. Nickelodeon, Splat and all related titles,
logos and characters are trademarks of Viacom International Inc.

A CIP catalogue record for this book is available from the British Library

ISBN 978-1-84738-486-7

10 9 8 7 6 5 4 3 2 1

Printed by CPI Cox & Wyman, Reading, Berkshire RG1 8EX

Chapter 1

It was another beautiful morning on Queensland's Gold Coast. A light breeze was rustling the leaves of the palm trees, the sea was lapping the sun-drenched beaches ... and Emma Gilbert was standing as still as a statue in the middle of her bathroom.

Emma stared down at the bath. The water was flowing out of the tap and the bath was getting fuller and fuller, but Emma didn't move a muscle. *Just move!* she told herself. *Come on!* But she couldn't seem to make herself get into the water. The bubbles rose higher and higher in the bath. The thought of what would happen seemed to have made all her muscles seize up.

Emma rolled her eyes. If she didn't get in now, she was going to be late for school. She leaned forward and turned off the tap, then

stared into the water. It had never seemed like an enemy before, but now she almost felt frightened of it. *This is silly*, she told herself. *It's just water, and you know exactly what's going to happen.* She let out a controlled breath, as she did when she was preparing for a swimming contest. She slowly pulled off her pyjamas. Then she stepped into the bath and slipped into the warm water.

She counted to ten as she waited. The water bubbled around her and she felt the familiar tingling sensation in her legs. Next moment a long, scaly, golden tail was draped over the edge of the bath. Emma clutched the sides of the bath, trying to stay calm.

Since Emma had found the strange cave on Mako Island with her friends Cleo and Rikki, everything had changed. One minute she had been a cool, collected student, in training for the swimming regionals. Then something super-weird had happened in that cave, and now everything was different. She only had to be

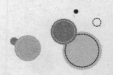

touched by a drop of water, and she grew a mermaid's tail. She could swim at hyper-speed. She could hold her breath for ten times longer than before. And with a wave of her hand she could turn water into solid ice.

Emma sighed and looked down at her long tail. It should have been so cool. But now, even taking a bath was a major risk. And she simply couldn't get used to it. Even though it had been days since their trip to Mako Island, she still hoped each time she got into the bath that *this* time, it wouldn't happen. *This* time the magic would have worn off, and she would be back to normal.

Emma wiggled her tail. It was lucky that her bath was in the middle of the room. Her tail was so long that it was almost touching the wall anyway. Emma leaned her head back and gazed at the ceiling, her face expressionless. This had happened every day since her visit to Mako Island, and she didn't think she was ever going to get used to it.

Not far away, Cleo Sertori was standing in front of her fish tank wearing a pair of pink washing-up gloves. She was wearing her most determined expression. The fish tank *had* to be cleaned, but it was a dangerous operation. If she stayed dry, there would be no problem. If she got wet … well, *that* was different story.

She took a deep breath and reached into the fish tank. Her hand dived deeper and deeper towards the clownfish that were swimming backwards and forwards. She twisted her hand to try to reach one, but it swerved out of her reach. Cleo wasn't paying attention to her hand. She reached further into the tank, stretching her fingers towards the fish. Then she felt a cold, wet sensation on her wrist, and her eyes widened. She gasped as water poured in over the top of her glove. Cleo's hand was soaked.

"Oh no!" she cried, feeling the water seep into the fingers of the glove, under her fingernails, into the very pores of her skin. "No, no, no, no, no, no!"

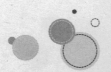

Quickly she tore off the gloves and grabbed a towel, rubbing her hands and arms in a mad panic. She had to dry the water off before it took effect! Her heart hammered – would she be quick enough? Then she heard a loud knock on the door.

"Cleo!" her sister Kim yelled. "Cleo!"

Cleo was distracted for a split second and failed to dry a few last drops of water that clung to her arm. Then she felt a tingling in her legs and knew that it was too late. She looked down and groaned as her legs turned into a tail.

Cleo flopped backwards onto her bed. Outside, Kim hammered on the door, her face wrinkled into a frown.

"Cleo!" she shouted again. "Dad says you have to hurry up if you want a lift to school."

"It's okay, Kim," Cleo answered, trying to keep the frustration out of her voice. "I'll walk."

Kim left to go to school, and Cleo reached over to her bedside table for her mobile phone.

She quickly texted a certain picture to Emma and Rikki. Since they had become mermaids, there had been several incidents just like this. They had realized that they needed some sort of sign – an alarm if any of them got into trouble. The picture they had chosen seemed to fit perfectly.

Over at Emma's house, her mother was just finishing the washing up when she heard Emma's phone beep.

"Em!" she called, drying her hands and walking over. "Your phone!"

She picked up the phone and checked the message. There was no text – just a picture of a clownfish. Emma's mother raised her eyebrows and shrugged. *Teenagers*, she thought. *I just don't understand them sometimes!*

On the beach, Rikki Chadwick's phone beeped with the same message. But there was no one

there to hear it. Rikki's phone was on her towel, waiting on the rocks. The waves were breaking in frothy white crests on the blue ocean. But the beach was deserted – Rikki was far out to sea, trying out her brand new swimming skills.

Rikki cut through the water with the graceful movements of a seal. Her arms were stretched out in front of her, and her long blonde hair flowed through the water, as bright as the sun. A huge smile was lighting up her face. She loved being underwater. Here, the world was quiet and welcoming. No one was judging her or asking her to change. Rikki loved the feeling of her strong body and firm muscles undulating through the ocean. There was no need for her to put on an act here. At school she was still the new kid, and she definitely didn't fit in with all the other squealing, image-obsessed girls. Since meeting Cleo and Emma, she had found some real friends, and now they shared their mermaid secret, they were closer than ever. But Rikki couldn't understand why they weren't thrilled about being mermaids. For her, it was a dream

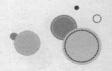

come true. Whenever she wanted, she could slip into a new world and escape from everyone and everything. *Who wouldn't want this?* she asked herself as she flicked her golden tail.

Rikki swam past fish of every size and shape. She felt as though she could never get tired of this. A curious dolphin saw her and came closer to investigate, clicking and squeaking in its own wonderful language. With a smile of pure delight, Rikki followed it. The dolphin rolled in the water, inviting her to play.

Rikki knew that she was going to be late for school, but she really didn't care. *Play with a dolphin or sit through a geography lesson*, she thought. *Some choice!* She followed the dolphin, copying its rolls and twists in the ocean. *I am completely free!* she thought. It was the best feeling in the world!

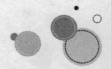

Chapter 2

"This is a catastrophe of the highest order!" said Cleo, walking out of the bathroom. Her face was full of alarm as she stared at her friends. Emma was sitting on the end of Cleo's bed looking concerned, and Rikki was lying across it, with absolutely no expression.

They had both raced over to Cleo's house when they had received her clownfish message. But in her imagination, Rikki was still darting through the water with the dolphin she had been playing with that morning, trying out her new skills. She didn't want to think about catastrophes.

Emma's thoughts were a little preoccupied too, but she raised her eyebrows expectantly. *Cleo must have found out something really serious*, she thought. Right now she would welcome anything that would take her thoughts

9

away from her swimming training. Then Cleo held up a tube of moisturizer and pointed at it.

"Moisturizer is mainly water!" Cleo wailed.

Emma slowly turned her head to look at Rikki. She knew that Cleo was always blowing things out of proportion, but this was ridiculous. She could already guess what Rikki would think of it. Emma bit her lip as Rikki opened her mouth to speak. She knew how easy it was to hurt Cleo's feelings.

Rikki was trying hard not to react badly, but patience was not her strong point, and the other two were really getting on her nerves. Cleo was so busy worrying over things like moisturizer, she hadn't even thought about all the cool stuff they could do now they had tails and could stay under water for so long. *And Emma's just as bad*, she thought. *All she can think about is her swimming championships. Don't they realize what an awesome gift this is?* She counted to ten and tried to focus on her own thoughts.

"If dolphins can swim for miles, so can we,"

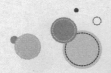

she said, visualising the young dolphin and remembering all the new moves she had learned from him. She was longing to get back into the water and test her limits.

"We can't moisturize *ever again!*" Cleo continued. *Don't they get how serious this is?* she asked herself.

Emma closed her eyes and tried to organize her thoughts. She *could* sympathize with Cleo. There would be hundreds of little things they wouldn't be able to do any more – this was going to totally change their lives. Perhaps moisturizer wasn't exactly high on her list of priorities, but that wasn't the point. That one moment on Mako Island was going to change the course of their lives forever, and Emma wasn't sure that she liked that idea *at all*.

Rikki's thoughts were heading in a completely different direction. An excited smile spread over her face, and she rolled over onto her stomach and sat up on the bed.

"We could swim all the way to Fiji," she said,

her eyes shining. "Could you imagine that?"

Emma had opened her eyes and was now staring fixedly at a pattern on Cleo's colourful quilt. She just couldn't feel the bubbling delight that Rikki could.

"Our skin will be dry and wrinkly!" Cleo shrieked, her voice getting higher and higher as she tried to make her friends see how awful the situation really was. "We'll be geriatrics by the time we're 21!"

Rikki stared at Cleo in disbelief, but Emma took a deep breath and gave a little nod.

"I missed training today," she said, her lips tightening. "First time in six years."

Rikki just rolled her eyes, but Cleo understood how much this meant to Emma. After all, she had helped her train – she knew that it was Emma's dream to become a champion swimmer.

"See," said Cleo, waving the tube of moisturizer in the air and sitting down on a

12

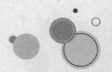

chair. "See how bad this is? We have to tell somebody. Our parents ... a doctor ... the police?"

She spoke as though she was talking absolute sense, but her friends knew that she wasn't thinking it through.

"And end up a mermaid in a straitjacket *with* moisturized skin?" said Rikki, raising her eyebrows and opening her blue eyes as wide as she could. She tightened her lips and shook her head. "Forget it!" *Doesn't she understand what they would do to us?* she wondered.

People were always scared of anything that was unusual or couldn't be explained. Cleo thought that they would be able to carry on with their lives as if nothing had changed, but Rikki knew that if anyone found out, they would never be left alone.

Cleo was annoyed. *Why can't Rikki see sense?* she thought. *She's so stubborn!*

Emma had been listening carefully and thinking hard. As much as she wanted to believe

that telling someone would solve all their problems, she knew that it would only make things worse. She got up off the bed and walked over to Cleo.

"Rikki's right, Cleo," she said gently, looking down at her. "We can't tell anyone."

Cleo stared at her, feeling very suspicious. They had been best friends for years, and Cleo had always listened to Emma and followed her lead. She trusted Emma to talk common sense, so if Emma agreed with Rikki, they must be right. Even so, it was very hard to believe. Cleo swallowed a few times and thought about what she was being asked to do.

"Not even Mum?" she suggested eventually, hoping to find a loophole.

"No," said Emma, shaking her head. "No parents."

"But I tell Mum everything," said Cleo, with a little smile. Surely Emma could understand that?

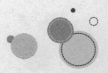

"Well, not this time," said Emma, her voice firm.

She felt sorry for Cleo, because she knew how hard it would be for her best friend to keep this to herself. But she had to find a way, or they could all be in serious trouble. Cleo was staring at her with an expression of disbelief.

"It's too dangerous," Emma said, trying to make her friend see her point of view. "People just won't understand. We could be locked up."

"Why would we be locked up?" asked Cleo. She could hardly believe her ears.

"Because we're different," Emma replied. "Because we can do things that other girls can't do. Because they're scared of us."

Emma knew that Cleo was scared of keeping such a big secret from her family and her other friends. Cleo looked down at her hands in her lap for a moment. Then she gave a little shrug, and Emma realized that the message was finally starting to get through.

"Fine," said Cleo. "I won't tell anyone." A smile curled up the side of her mouth. "Except Lewis."

She felt happy to have made this decision – it seemed like a fair compromise. She could keep the secret if she could just tell *one* person. Lewis wouldn't tell anyone, Cleo was sure of that.

But Rikki rolled her eyes. She had kept quiet while Emma was speaking, knowing that Emma had the best chance of persuading Cleo to keep this quiet. But she couldn't sit and listen while they went round in circles. Why was Cleo being so dense about this?

"No, Cleo," she said, thoroughly exasperated. "Not Lewis, not *anyone*."

She sounds like she's talking to a child, Cleo thought in irritation. She looked up at Emma, but she could see that for once, Emma and Rikki were in complete agreement.

"Okay, okay," said Cleo finally. She smiled sweetly at her two friends. "Don't worry! I'm *really* good at keeping secrets."

Rikki pursed up her mouth and scratched the back of her head. *I'm not so sure about that*, she thought. Cleo stood up and threw the tube of moisturizer into the bin. Rikki stared at her, and then looked up at Emma, who had the same doubtful expression on her face. One thing was certain – they were going to have to watch Cleo like hawks.

Chapter 3

The sun was shining down on the school as the bell rang shrilly. Everyone filed out of their classrooms and headed for their lockers. They had a ten-minute break between classes – just enough time to grab their books for the next class and exchange a little gossip. The school corridors were bustling with students jostling their way through, chatting, arguing and laughing.

Miriam, the school's resident golden girl, strolled down the main corridor as if she owned it, handing out invitations and giving orders at the top of her voice. No one got in Miriam's way – they wouldn't dare.

"Now, it's party time, people, no excuses," she announced. "In honour of our very own surfing god, the beautiful Byron, for winning his special prize."

She exchanged a smug smile with her friend Tiffany. Actually, 'friend' wasn't quite the right description. Tiffany wasn't as pretty, rich or confident as Miriam, and that was why Miriam hung around with her. Tiffany was there to remind Miriam of how fabulous Miriam was.

Miriam was pretty, with her sleek blonde hair and her flawless skin, but her looks were spoiled by the sour, superior expression she always wore. There was no warmth in her eyes, and she made friends with people on the basis of how popular they were. Byron had won a prize and was very popular. Therefore he was worthy of attention.

Tiffany kept handing out invitations as Miriam stopped next to the lockers and struck a pose. Rikki and Emma looked up apprehensively from their lockers. They really didn't want to spend their time talking about some snooty party with the school's so-called Miss Popular. Rikki glowered at Miriam and Emma glanced over at Cleo, hoping that she

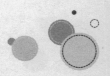

wouldn't say anything and start a conversation.

But Cleo loved parties.

"What prize?" she asked.

"Whatever it is they give out for surfing," replied Miriam in a bored voice, vaguely waving her hand in the air. She didn't really care; to her it was just another excuse to have a party and be the centre of attention.

Her attitude totally sucks, thought Emma. She knew how much work and dedication went into achieving your goals, and she knew how hard Byron had trained and practised. *Miriam has never even noticed him before*, she thought angrily. *Now all of a sudden he's a success, and that makes him fair game.*

Here she was, talking as if she owned Byron, and she couldn't even be bothered to find out what he had won. Emma didn't want to get involved in this conversation, but she couldn't keep quiet.

"The Coast Surf Classic," she said, looking at

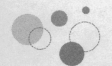

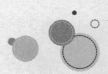

Cleo and trying to ignore Miriam. "He won by a mile."

Emma had been one of the first on the beach to watch the competition, and she had yelled herself hoarse and cheered with the crowd as Byron had surfed his way to the Coast Surf Classic. It had been an awesome day and Byron totally deserved all the praise he was getting. *I just don't see why Miriam thinks she should have a piece of it*, Emma thought.

She turned back to her locker, hoping that Miriam would take the hint, move on and bother someone else. But Miriam never reacted to subtle hints. Either she didn't notice them or she just really didn't care. She gave Emma her best *whatever* expression.

"I was having a spray tan, but I'm sure he was amazing," she said, completely uninterested.

Now it was Rikki's turn to look her up and down with an expression of utter disgust. *What sort of stupid, girly, empty-headed idiot gets a spray tan when they live on the Gold Coast?* she

thought. She was about to say the same thing out loud when Miriam caught her gaze and looked down at the party invitations in her hand.

"Rikki," she said, pretending to shuffle through the pile of invitations. "I'm sure I might have a blank ... um ..."

She looked up with a smirk. It was obvious that she didn't have an invitation for Rikki and she wanted to make sure that Rikki knew it. Emma shook her head. How was Miriam able to make people feel small even when her words seemed friendly?

But Rikki didn't mind. She didn't want to hang out with the so-called 'cool kids'. She thought they were lame, and she also thought that Miriam needed to be taught a few lessons.

"Sorry, I'll be flossing my teeth that night," said Rikki, shrugging and screwing up her nose as if Miriam was a bad smell.

Miriam raised her eyebrows in irritation. It always annoyed her when someone stood up to her. She glanced over at Tiffany and rolled her

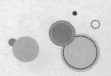

eyes. Together they flounced off down the corridor.

Emma and Rikki closed their lockers and headed off to their next class, both agreeing what an idiot Miriam was. Cleo was about to follow them when her friend Lewis McCartney walked past and saw her shutting her locker door.

"Oh, hey Cleo," he said.

He hurried over to her, smiling.

"Hey Lewis," said Cleo, turning to him and smiling back. She was just thinking about what news she had to tell him when she remembered her promise to Rikki and Emma. *This is the perfect chance to show how great I am at keeping secrets!* she thought. She made her expression as open and trustworthy as she could.

Lewis frowned slightly. Why was Cleo giving him such a weird look?

"Nothing much has been happening with me, nothing much at all," said Cleo. "Just the same

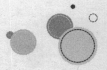

old thing."

This keeping a secret thing is easy, she thought, pleased with herself.

What on earth is she talking about? Lewis wondered.

"Cleo, er …" Lewis stammered, feeling mildly puzzled and then deciding that it was probably just Cleo being Cleo, "… er, are you going to Miriam's party?"

"Of course I'm going," replied Cleo quickly. She had never been known to miss a party!

She beamed at Lewis and he smiled back hopefully, opening his mouth to speak. Just at that moment, Miriam walked past again.

"Now don't forget, girls, bring your best bikinis," she said, as if she was talking to a bunch of five-year-olds. "It's a pool party!"

She swept off down the corridor with Tiffany trailing along in her wake.

Cleo's heart sank. She couldn't believe it. *There's no way I can go to a pool party,* she

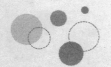
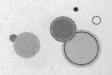

thought. *If I get wet, I'll blow it and grow a stupid mermaid tail and look like a freak!* There was only one thing for it – she was going to have to miss one of Miriam's parties for the first time *ever*.

"Right … ahhh … well, seeing as you're going …" began Lewis, trying to pluck up his courage. He could feel his cheeks going red as he searched for the right words, but as he opened his mouth, Cleo interrupted him.

"I've changed my mind," said Cleo, "I'm not going." *And I'll never be invited anywhere again!* she added to herself as she walked off to her next class.

She didn't see Lewis's expression as he stood and watched her go. Cleo was always a little bit … different … but she had never changed her mind that fast before. Lewis swallowed hard and felt very small. Had she guessed what he was about to say and not wanted to hear it? His shoulders slumped and he shuffled away to class.

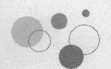

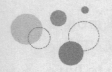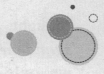

Chapter 4

Cleo didn't stop talking about Miriam's party all day. She whispered about it to Rikki in English. She moaned about it all the way through Media Studies, and she made Emma miss half her History lesson by sending her secret notes about it. She spent the whole of their lunch break speculating about what everyone would be wearing, and she doodled mermaid tails all over her Maths book until Rikki noticed and ripped the offending pages out, for which she received a detention.

By the end of the day, Rikki and Emma felt as if they never wanted to hear the word 'party' again. They left school together and headed down the path towards the sea, enjoying the afternoon sun beating down on their faces. For a while it seemed as though Cleo must have got over her desire to go to the party. They talked

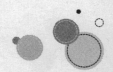

about their homework and gossiped about who was definitely dating whom in their class. But as they passed the sprinkler where Rikki had first discovered her tail, Cleo started again. She skipped ahead of them a few steps and then turned to face them, walking backwards.

"It's so uncool to miss one of Miriam's parties," she said. "She won't ask us *ever* again."

"So?" snapped Rikki, who wasn't sure how much more of this she could take. "That's a *plus*."

Why does Cleo want to go to a party like that anyway? Rikki asked herself. *Miriam's totally horrible. Parties like that are never any fun.*

"It's a *pool* party," Cleo said, turning around again and ignoring Rikki. Surely her friends could see that one little pool party wouldn't be a problem if they were properly prepared? Besides, she had an idea. "I *know* it's dangerous," she began, "but … maybe if I told Lewis about us he could look out for us?"

"No!" said Rikki. "You did the right thing,

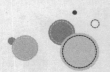

Cleo. None of us are going."

She was tired of explaining to Cleo why they had to keep quiet about this mermaid situation. They couldn't go to a boring, stuck-up pool party. So what? Rikki had spent her first few weeks at the school hardly speaking to anyone. Now she had two good friends, she didn't need any more.

Cleo folded her arms and the corners of her mouth drooped. But then Emma spoke up. She had been thinking about this all day (with Cleo around, it had been impossible to think about anything else) and something was bothering her.

"No, wait," she said, stopping in her tracks. "I think we should go."

The other two girls stopped as well, and turned to her. Rikki stared at her in amazement. Cleo looked delighted. They waited for further explanation.

"For Byron, not for Miriam," Emma explained, her head on one side. "Surfing is just like swimming – it takes a lot of hard work and

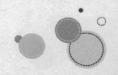

training. You need to know everyone is supporting you."

Emma smiled at them, feeling that she had explained herself very well. But then a knowing grin spread over Rikki's face. Emma waited, feeling very apprehensive. That was the trouble with Rikki – you never knew what she was going to say.

"You *like* Byron, don't you?" Rikki asked in a singsong voice, her eyes twinkling.

Cleo looked at Rikki and grinned. She loved the way that Rikki was never scared to speak her mind.

"No way," replied Emma, smiling as if it was the most ridiculous idea in the world. But Cleo and Rikki noticed that Emma didn't meet their eyes, and she started to walk on as if she suddenly wanted to get away from the conversation.

"Well, you sound like an ad for breakfast cereal," scoffed Rikki, shrugging her shoulders and following Emma.

"Well," said Emma, desperately trying to move the conversation away from this tricky topic and back to safer ground, "if we learn more about what's happening to us, we might be able to control it enough to go to the party."

She wasn't entirely sure what she meant, but Cleo seized on the suggestion eagerly.

"Really?" she gasped in excitement.

Cleo looked at her best friend in admiration. There had never been anything Emma couldn't do if she set her mind to it. Perhaps they would be able to go after all! She really valued Emma's cool intelligence and her ability to think things through cleverly. Cleo felt sure that if anyone could find a solution to this problem, it was Emma.

Rikki was not so happy. She thought that Emma was grasping at straws, and she definitely didn't like the thought of Cleo turning up at a pool party.

"What's to learn?" she enquired, throwing out her arms in amazement. "We touch water

and ten seconds later we grow tails!" *Not Emma too*! she thought. *Is everyone in this town obsessed with stuck-up, popular girls and lame pool parties?*

"Maybe it's about developing some discipline, exercising some control," said Emma.

Rikki scowled at her, but Cleo was nodding happily.

"That'd be perfect," she said, without the slightest idea of what Emma was talking about. "That's great! Control. Then we can go to the party!" She pulled her phone out of her bag. "I'll text Lewis."

She quickly tapped out a message, telling him that she would be going to the party after all. She pressed 'send' and smiled. But Rikki had been watching her and thinking. Her frown cleared and she looked expectantly at Cleo. She was starting to understand that Cleo never thought things through. She was willing to bet that there was one thing Cleo hadn't considered.

"You do realize you're going to have swim to

test this theory?" she asked.

"What?" cried Cleo, looking at Emma, who nodded in agreement. "No way. Forget it."

She shoved her phone back into her bag. Cleo had always been scared of the water and she had never even learned to swim. Even the hope of a party couldn't make her change her mind. The only time she had been in the sea was when they had finally escaped from Mako Island, and that had almost scared her out of her wits – not to mention all the trouble it had caused.

No way, she thought. *I'm never setting a toenail in the sea ever again!*

She marched on ahead and Emma exchanged a glance with Rikki. This was going to take a very long time.

From the first moment that she had accepted that she was a mermaid, Emma had known that they somehow had to persuade Cleo to get into the water and help them to work out what was happening. Because Cleo was so scared of the

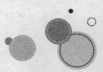

water, up till now Emma and Rikki had been the ones to go exploring in the ocean. They had had a truly amazing time. They had spent hours testing how fast they could swim, exploring the seabed and meeting underwater creatures. They had visited reefs and discovered wonderful new abilities. It had been like visiting another world, and Emma wished Cleo could see it too.

She thought that perhaps the party would be the incentive Cleo needed to finally get into the water. *I'm sure she'll love it when she actually gives it a try*, Emma thought.

Rikki was thinking hard. Although she couldn't care less about the party, she thought that it would be a really good idea to see if there *was* more to find out about what was happening to them. Even though she loved being a mermaid, she privately had to admit that it could be very inconvenient not to be able to control the change. She followed Cleo, imagining how cool it would be to be able to decide exactly when she turned into a mermaid. This idea of Emma's was definitely worth a try.

33

She hurried to catch up with Cleo and slipped an arm through hers, grinning at her. Between her and Emma, she was sure they could persuade Cleo to head down to the beach with them.

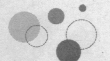
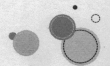

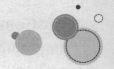

Chapter 5

A short while later, the three friends were down on the beach in the most secret, secluded spot they could find. It was a place that Lewis had once told Cleo about. Emma and Rikki had begged and pleaded with Cleo to join them, and eventually she had told them about this place and had even agreed to come down to the water with them. But as soon as she saw the blue ocean stretching all the way out to the horizon, and heard the waves splashing onto the sand, she had frozen. She sat on some rocks, hugged her legs to her chest and buried her head in her knees.

Rikki stood in front of Cleo, her hands on her hips. Emma was beside her with her arms folded. Rikki had put on her bikini and Emma was in a singlet top and shorts, but Cleo had refused point-blank to get changed.

"Come *on*," pleaded Rikki for the umpteenth time. "It's not even deep here."

"No," said Cleo, looking up and shaking her head. They had persuaded her to get into the water when they had been stuck in that cave, but that was because they hadn't had a choice. This time Cleo was safely on dry land, and that was where she intended to stay.

"Please, Cleo," pleaded Rikki.

"No," said Cleo, looking from Rikki to Emma. "*No*!"

"*Fine*," said Emma, exasperated. "Come on, Rikki."

She realized that getting her best friend into the water was as impossible as trying to move one of the rocks that Cleo was sitting on. They were going to have to *show* her that there was nothing to worry about!

Cleo felt awful. She knew that her friends were annoyed with her, but she just couldn't bring herself to do what they wanted. Why *can't*

they understand how scary this is for me? she thought. She watched Emma and Rikki stride down to the shoreline and felt thoroughly unhappy.

Emma and Rikki were feeling nervous too, but each of them was determined not to give in to it. They had to start looking for answers, and they would do whatever it took to reach an understanding of what had happened to them.

"Control and discipline start with the mind, so ... concentrate," Emma told Rikki.

They reached the water's edge and waded into the shallow waves that lapped the sandy beach. Then they turned and faced Cleo, who was squinting in the sun. They all knew that whatever had happened to them on Mako Island had done more than just give them tails. Emma and Cleo could both control water with their thoughts, and although Rikki didn't seem to have a power like that, who knew what might

happen when they started concentrating their minds?

They were both nervous, but they had to hide it from Cleo. Rikki wasn't sure what Emma had in mind, but she decided that she would just watch and copy whatever her friend did.

Emma wasn't entirely sure what her plan was either, but she could sense that Rikki was following her lead. She started to use a focusing technique that her swimming coach had taught her, closing her eyes and chanting instructions to her body over and over again. Her body had always done what she wanted it to do before. Just because she had a tail, why should that be any different?

"No tail, no tail, no tail," Emma intoned. "No tail, no tail …"

Rikki looked sideways at her and then joined in. "No tail, no tail, no ta–"

They broke off as their legs started to tingle and blue sparkles crept up their bodies. Then they tumbled into the sea, thrashing their tails

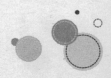

helplessly. It was no good. No amount of control was going to make any difference! They looked at each other and sighed. It took a long time to dry off in the sun – now they would have to lie on the rocks and wait until their legs came back before they could try again.

Cleo watched them from the beach. She hadn't seen her friends transform before, and her mouth dropped open a little. Just like when she transformed, Rikki and Emma had developed long, golden, scaly tails. Their skin glowed slightly and their hair was flowing loose and free. For a split second, Cleo forgot her fears and just thought how amazing they looked. Then her heart plummeted. If even Emma couldn't control this thing, what hope was there for *her*?

What are we going to do? she thought. *Nothing is going to work! I don't want to have to stay at home for the rest of my life because I might get a drop of water on myself!*

Suddenly, Rikki gave a horrified double take. Behind Cleo, Lewis was walking down the beach towards them, carrying a load of fishing gear!

Rikki cast a terrified look at Emma, who spotted him at exactly the same moment. They dragged themselves behind a rock just in time. Lewis spotted them looking out from behind the rock and strolled over.

"Who leaked the information?" he demanded jokingly.

Cleo, who had been staring out to sea with her arms folded, turned around in shock at the sound of his voice. She looked him up and down, taking in his fishing rod, his box and his fisherman's hat. For a moment she was completely lost for words.

"This is my secret, highly classified fishing spot," Lewis continued, coming right down onto the rocks beside her. He looked at Rikki and Emma, whose heads were poking out above the rocks. "Someone must've blabbed."

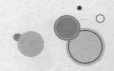

"Sorry," said Cleo, willing him to leave with every fibre of her being. Why had he chosen *this* moment to go fishing? She looked at her friends, who were both wearing identical horrified expressions.

"That's fine," said Lewis cheerfully. "Hey, I got your message about going to the party."

Oh no! thought Cleo. *I forgot all about that!* After watching Emma and Rikki trying to control their mermaid-ness in the sea, there was absolutely no way she was going to be able to attend Miriam's party.

"Oh, that was an old message," she said, trying to think of a better explanation – and failing. "I'm not going any more – too much homework."

I hope he falls for that, she thought to herself, although it seemed an unbelievably lame excuse.

"Fine," said Lewis, who didn't seem to notice Cleo's discomfort. He put down his fishing rod and started to unbutton his shirt. "Well, I might just join you all for a swim, then."

Behind the rock, Rikki and Emma looked at each other in terror – what could they do? If Lewis got much closer he would see them for what they really were!

"We're naked, Lewis," said Rikki, blurting out the first thing she thought of.

Emma nodded in agreement, for once feeling very glad of Rikki and her big mouth. *Sometimes she has the best ideas!* Emma thought. Even in the middle of danger, she couldn't help feeling amused when she saw Lewis's expression. His smile had become very fixed. He looked out to sea thoughtfully and then shrugged his shoulders.

"Just a quick dip then?" he suggested finally.

"Goodbye, Lewis," said Emma.

Lewis did up his buttons again, and then bent down and picked up his fishing gear.

"The offer was there," he said, implying that they had missed the opportunity of a lifetime.

He walked away up the beach and Cleo let

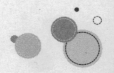

out a long sigh of relief. Emma grinned at Rikki, who raised her eyebrows and tapped her fingers on the rock. That had been a little too close for comfort!

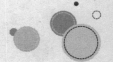

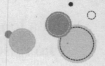

Chapter 6

Emma and Rikki waited for the sun to dry them off and then tried again. They focused as hard as they could, visualising their legs and ordering their tails not to appear. But it didn't seem to matter how hard they concentrated or how many times they tried. It made absolutely no difference at all. Eventually they were all getting hungry and thirsty, and they had to give up.

Hot and tired after their near-discovery by Lewis and their efforts at the beach, the girls went to Emma's house for some rest and refreshment. There was no one home and they needed to come up with another plan if they were ever going to have any control over their lives. Emma and Cleo walked into the kitchen, their shoulders slumped and their expressions depressed. It had been a very demoralising afternoon for them all.

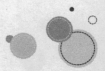

"We're never going to be invited anywhere cool ever again," said Cleo, who was still focusing on the party. "And why? Because we've got *tails*."

She pulled a glass from the draining board, poured herself a drink of water from the cooler and banged it down on the counter. Rikki leaned back against the breakfast bar and watched her.

"My swimming career is *over*," Emma added. Usually she would have tried to look for the positive in the situation, but right now it didn't seem as if this situation *had* any positives.

She opened the fridge and leaned on the door for a moment, staring moodily into it. Nothing seemed very appealing. Finally she reached in and pulled out the jug of orange juice. She knew exactly how Cleo felt. For her, it was as if everything she had been working for was slipping away. She thought of all those mornings when she had got up early to go to swimming training before school. They were all

wasted! Her whole life had been about swimming, and now she couldn't even go *near* the water. It was all so unfair.

Emma poured some orange juice into a glass, grabbed an icy pole stick from the drawer and flopped down next to Rikki at the breakfast bar. She knew she was whinging, and it had always driven her mad when Cleo did it. *But why shouldn't I whinge?* she thought. *Haven't I got something to whinge about? All my plans and hopes have been totally shattered.*

Rikki looked up at the ceiling as her friends went quiet. *Is that it?* she wondered. *Have they finally stopped moaning?* Emma and Cleo had done nothing but complain all the way back from the beach. They hadn't even seemed to notice how quiet Rikki had become. They were too busy wailing about how awful their lives were – and Rikki was rapidly getting sick of it. *Okay, so things are different*, she thought. *Different is good! Different is exciting!*

"I have just one question," Cleo went on,

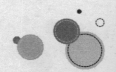

glaring at her glass of water as though it was to blame. "Why me? I didn't ask for any of this to happen."

Rikki's expression grew even darker. *Will they never stop*? she asked herself. She watched as Cleo flicked her hand at the glass of water. A bubble of water popped out of the glass and hovered over it. Cleo used her power to make the bubble rise into the air until it was hovering next to her head. Then she leaned in and closed her mouth around it, swallowing as if it was the most ordinary thing in the world. Rikki opened her mouth to say something and then closed it again.

"You think *you've* got problems!" Emma moaned. "I've been training to be a swimmer since I was six months old."

She stirred her drink with the icy pole stick and then, holding it in the middle of the glass, used her power to freeze the orange juice and make herself an icy pole. She pulled the icy pole out of the glass, looked at it critically for a

47

moment, and then licked it with an absent-minded expression.

"Well say goodbye to those dreams, because we're mer-freaks now," said Cleo.

Rikki was looking from one of them to the other in absolute amazement. She hated to lose her cool, but she just couldn't stay laid-back when her friends were being so blind. After everything they had done and seen, how could they still be acting as if this was the biggest tragedy of all time?

"You two are *unbelievable*," she said. "Look at yourselves!" She glared at Cleo. "You're drinking water from *mid-air*." She walked around the breakfast bar. "And Emma, you just made an instant icy pole." She paused for a moment to let her words sink in. "Anybody else would *love* to be able to do that."

Including me, she thought. She stopped next to Emma and glared at her. She almost felt more annoyed with Emma. Cleo had been too scared to come into the water, but Emma had swum

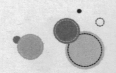

through the ocean alongside Rikki. She had played with dolphins and explored reefs. When they had come out of the water, she had been just as amazed and delighted as Rikki. They had walked back to Emma's house bubbling over with excitement about what they had just done. Now it was as if all that had never happened.

Emma glanced at Cleo, feeling slightly ashamed of herself. Cleo was looking exactly like she did when a teacher told her off at school. Neither of them wanted to meet Rikki's accusing gaze.

"You've both got these amazing powers and all you do is whinge, whinge, *whinge*," Rikki went on. "I don't even *have* a power. Do you hear me complaining?"

Cleo shrugged her shoulders and gave a little shake of her head. She felt embarrassed. Rikki was right, she had been whinging a lot, but then her life *was* over, socially speaking.

"No," said Rikki, confirming Cleo's shake of the head. She paused for a moment, but neither

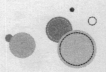

of her friends seemed to want to say anything.

Emma was completely lost for words. She had never been spoken to like that, and she felt as if she ought to be angry. The trouble was, she had a sneaking suspicion that Rikki might actually have a point. Cleo didn't know what to say either. She felt her cheeks growing pink as Rikki's eyes bored into hers. *That girl certainly knows how to give looks!* she thought.

Rikki had thought that her friends would reply, but they were just staring at her like idiots. She was thoroughly fed up. Her temper flared and her eyes blazed.

"Well, I've had enough," she announced. "I don't want to hang around with whingers."

She raised her eyebrows at them and then turned and walked out of the kitchen, up the steps and into the hall. She wrenched open the door without pausing and yanked it shut behind her. *I'd rather be on my own than have to put up with listening to that!* she thought, fuming.

Emma and Cleo heard the front door slam

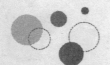

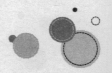

and then turned to look at each other. Cleo squirmed and looked down at the kitchen floor.

"I know how she feels," she said eventually. "Sometimes *I* don't even want to hang around with me."

Emma stared at her and then looked at her orange icy pole. As much as she hated to admit it, she knew that Rikki was right. Instead of moaning about what they had lost, they had to start enjoying what they *had*. It was time to accept the fact that things were different now. She just hoped that they hadn't lost a friend forever.

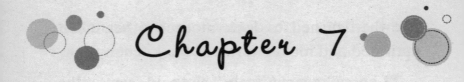

Chapter 7

Cleo didn't stay at Emma's house very long after Rikki had stormed out. Emma seemed really preoccupied, and Cleo still felt a little embarrassed about what Rikki had said. She texted Lewis and arranged to meet him at the Juice-Net Café. After she left Emma's, she hurried down to the beach, over the little bridge and into the café. Lewis was already there waiting for her when she walked in.

Lewis is such a great friend, Cleo thought as she walked towards him. She loved all her friends, but sometimes Rikki acted as if she thought Cleo was really silly. Emma could be a bit too bossy occasionally. But Lewis always listened to her as if what she said was really important. He wasn't impatient or demanding. He was just … well … he was just Lewis. Cleo really valued his opinion, and she suddenly decided that it would be really interesting to

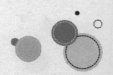

know what he thought about the argument earlier.

"Lewis," began Cleo as she took a seat at the table where he sat. "What do you think of Rikki?"

Lewis put his head on one side and considered the question. He didn't want to sound like a wimp … but he didn't want to lie either.

"You know those stonefish that kind of look like a rock?" he said after a moment's thought. "Yet can shoot enough poison to kill an entire football team in half a second? She kind of reminds me of one of those."

Before Cleo could think about how to explain what had happened earlier without mentioning mermaids or tails, Byron, the local surfing champ, walked in. He was followed by Zane Bennett and some other kids that Cleo recognized from school.

Everyone in the café burst into applause, including Cleo. She stood up and walked over

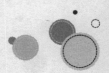

towards Byron, while Lewis watched.

"Thanks guys," said Byron as the people in the Juice-Net Café kept clapping. He grinned and his tanned face lit up with a smile. He didn't surf in order to be popular – he surfed because he loved it. It was really nice of everyone to want to congratulate him … he just hoped all this attention wasn't going to last too long. "Hey – relax," he added, starting to get embarrassed.

Cleo stopped next to Byron and smiled at him. She was wishing all over again that she could go to Miriam's party. Byron was such a cool guy and she would really like to get to know him better. Instead she'd have to mope around at home. *A pool party!* she thought. *Of all the stupid ideas! How could Miriam be so dumb?*

"Congratulations, Byron," she said. "What's your ranking now? You must be getting up there."

Byron shrugged modestly and was about to answer when Zane interrupted.

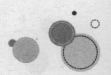

"Control yourself," he snarled, making it sound as though Cleo was throwing herself at Byron.

Zane was still angry with Cleo. Only a few days earlier he had set her adrift in his boat for a joke, only to have the Water Police turn up at his house and embarrass him in front of his dad. When he had tried to confront her about it, a fire hydrant had exploded and the jet of water had knocked him off his feet, totally drenching and humiliating him. He didn't know that Cleo had used her powers to control the fire hydrant, but he did know that she had made him look like an idiot, and he wanted to get his own back.

Lewis had been watching and listening. As soon as he saw that Cleo was upset he spoke up, trying to divert Zane's attention away from his friend. He hated seeing Cleo get picked on.

"Hey Zane, you're *dry*," he called from his table in a fake friendly voice. "That must feel different."

It worked. Zane barged over to Lewis's table

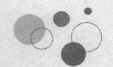

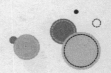

and leaned over him in a threatening pose, his lip curling with fury.

"Look, Lewis," said Zane in a low, menacing growl. "I don't know what happened with that fire hydrant, but if you so much as mention it again, I'll remove your head from your shoulders."

Zane turned away and Lewis frowned. He wasn't a coward, and he wasn't going to sit there and take being threatened by a thug like Zane Bennett. Lewis jumped up from his seat and clamped his hand down on Zane's shoulder. If Zane wanted a fight, he could have one! Zane turned and looked down at Lewis's hand. Then his eyes travelled back up to Lewis's face, flashing furiously.

Byron and the other kids had turned away, but Cleo saw what was happening. She didn't want to see Lewis get hurt, and she knew that he was no fighter. She could feel her heart pounding.

"Let it go, Lewis," she begged.

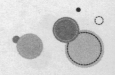

Byron whipped his head around and instantly took in the scene. Lewis gave Zane's shoulder a little shove and released it. Byron walked over to them, his usually cheerful face suddenly serious.

"She's right, he's not worth it, mate," said Byron to Lewis. He looked at Zane and shook his head. "Will it change him? No."

By this time a little group had gathered around Lewis and Zane, and Wilfred, the owner of the Juice-Net Café, had noticed what was going on. He strode over to Zane and pulled him to one side. He was very easy-going with the kids who came into his café, but he wouldn't put up with fighting, and this wasn't the first time he'd had to speak to Zane.

The others watched as Wilfred led Zane away from them. He sat the boy down and proceeded to give him a telling off that made Zane's ears go pink with embarrassment. He glowered at Cleo. This was the third time in a week she had made him look like a complete

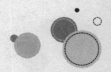

fool. Sooner or later, he was going to teach her a lesson she'd never forget.

Byron went to talk to some friends and Cleo sat back down with Lewis, oblivious to Zane's glares.

"Byron is *such* a nice guy," said Cleo.

Lewis stabbed his straw into his drink and stared fixedly into space. He didn't think he could cope with sitting there while Cleo raved about some other boy.

"Emma's right," Cleo continued. "We *should* go to Miriam's party to show some support for him."

Cleo was so busy thinking about how Byron had helped Lewis out that she didn't notice Lewis's expression. He turned to look at her as she carried on talking. She was so glad that Byron had stepped in when he did – she would have hated Lewis to get hurt because of her. Anything could have happened if he hadn't put a stop to it. *He didn't have to get involved, but he could see that Lewis was in danger*, she thought.

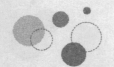

"I mean," she added aloud, a dreamy smile lighting up her face. "What a hero."

"Great!" said Lewis, who was now totally fed up. "So go."

"Do you think?" asked Cleo.

"Yeah, sure, whatever blows your hair back," he said with heavy sarcasm.

Cleo suddenly realized that Lewis was not being his usual self. She stared at him in confusion, and he just glared back at her.

"Cleo, I don't get you," he said. "One minute you're going and then you're not and now you're going again!"

He shook his head, grabbed his hat and his drink, and marched out of the café. Cleo watched him go and let out a long sigh.

Oh dear, she thought. *I've managed to lose two friends in one day. That must be some kind of record!*

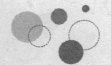

Chapter 8

Next morning, Emma was sitting at the breakfast bar eating cereal and staring into space. She had been lying awake half the night, thinking about her future, and she was still feeling terrible. She hadn't been able to exercise as normal and her body was missing it, but that wasn't the real problem. She had always been absolutely certain that her life would involve swimming. But now, after one spooky night on Mako Island, everything had changed. Without swimming, she had nothing. *Without swimming I am nothing*, she thought. She knew that Rikki had been right and she should put swimming to one side and get on with making a new life, but it really wasn't as easy as that. She could feel tears pricking her eyes and she angrily blinked them back. She dropped her spoon into her cereal bowl and sat with her head in her hands.

The front door closed with a bang. It was her

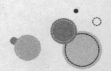

parents coming home from their early morning run. As they headed upstairs to get showered and ready for work, they saw Emma sitting at the breakfast bar and stopped, staring at her. Emma sat back up with a jump, picked up her bowl and started eating again as if nothing was wrong. She glanced up at her parents and tried to look normal.

"Are you *sure* you can afford to miss training again?" Emma's mum asked.

Emma's lips tightened and she took another spoonful of cereal, looking down at the bowl as if there was something fascinating in it. This was not a conversation she wanted to have right now.

"Aren't the regionals coming up?" added her dad, frowning slightly.

"You trained when you had the flu," added her mum. "Even when you broke your wrist — you swam with one arm."

Emma said nothing. *It's like being under attack*, she thought. *Just leave me alone!*

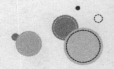

Her parents looked at each other. This was not the Emma they knew.

"If she's that bad, maybe she should see the doctor," said her dad, who could only think that Emma must be really ill.

"I don't need a doctor," said Emma quickly. That was the *last* thing she wanted!

Her dad shrugged and continued up the stairs, but her mum turned back and came into the kitchen. Emma sighed as her mum stopped next to her and looked down at her with real concern.

Emma took a long gulp of orange juice. *Go away, go away, go away*, she thought. She had never lied to her parents before, and although this wasn't exactly lying, it felt just as bad.

"Sweetheart," her mum began, "you have been spending an awful lot of time in your bedroom lately ... and ... locked up in the bathroom. Is there anything we need to talk about?"

Emma heard the worry in her mum's voice, but she couldn't tell her the truth. After all, she had made Cleo promise not to say anything to *her* parents. And there was no way her mother would understand. She had to act as if there was nothing wrong.

"It's nothing," she said, scooping up another spoonful of cereal and popping it into her mouth.

"It's all right to feel moody," said her mum.

Emma rolled her eyes. She knew exactly what was coming, and she really didn't need another talk about growing up! It had been embarrassing enough the first time around ...

"You're at an age where you're going through a lot of changes," her mum went on.

Oh, you have no idea how right you are, Emma thought. *I have to nip this conversation in the bud before it gets worse!*

"Exactly, Mum, got it in one," she said crisply. She grabbed her drink and slid off her

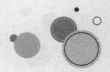

seat. She was out of the room before her mum could say another word. She was already feeling depressed about swimming and about her argument with Rikki. She didn't have any energy left to try to think of explanations for her parents.

Cleo had also had a sleepless night. She had tossed and turned, unable to stop thinking about Lewis and Rikki, and wondering whether she was ever going to be friends with them again. When she had finally managed to get to sleep, she had been plagued with nightmares in which Miriam threw water on her in the middle of school and she was lying on the classroom floor with a tail. Everyone was laughing at her, including Lewis, Rikki and Emma.

When she woke up, she could still hear the laughter ringing in her ears, and she knew that she had to do something. She couldn't let this mermaid thing wreck her social life forever. There had to be a way that she could protect her

64

secret and still go to the party. Perhaps if she only had a little bit of skin showing, she would be able to dry herself off before the ten seconds had passed.

That was why she was now standing in her bath, dressed in a wetsuit. She was also wearing a plastic shower cap and waterproof gloves. *This has just got to work!* she told herself. *Yes, this is the answer! I am going to be at that pool party if it's the last thing I do!*

She felt so confident that she picked up her phone and dialled Miriam's number. It was awkward in the thick waterproof gloves, but Cleo decided that it was all good practice. The phone rang a couple of times and then she heard Miriam's smooth voice at the other end.

"Hi Miriam," said Cleo in her most cheerful voice. "I was just calling to let you know I'll *definitely* be at your party ..." she paused for a moment, not wanting to tempt fate, and then added, "... probably."

Miriam was not impressed. She enquired

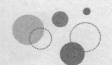

whether Cleo was going to start calling her *every* time she wasn't able to make up her mind about something.

"Well, I just thought I'd let you know," said Cleo, slightly offended.

Miriam, who was always bored by a conversation unless it was about her, began to describe her party bikini. Then she asked what Cleo would be wearing. She had to make sure that she wasn't outshone by anyone.

"What will I be wearing?" repeated Cleo, stalling for time. She looked down at her blue and black wetsuit and sighed. "Something appropriate."

Miriam made a noise like a cat sneezing and hung up. Cleo hung up too and rolled her eyes. *Yes, something appropriate*, she thought, imagining herself in a wetsuit at a pool party. *Still, better to be in a wetsuit at a pool party than not at a party at all!*

She put down her phone and picked up the bucket that she had filled with water. Then she

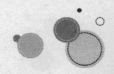

glanced at the little clock she had brought with her into the bathroom. Keeping one eye on the second hand, she lifted the bucket up high.

"*Go!*" she yelled, and tipped the bucket over her head.

As the water drenched her, she hopped out of the bath, grabbed a towel and began to dry herself off as fast as she could, counting out loud as she rubbed.

"Ten … nine …" she dried her face, "eight … seven … six …" she rubbed the towel over her arms, "five … four … three …" she began to dry her legs, "two … one … *ohhh*!"

She looked down in dismay as the now familiar blue glow swirled around her body. Then she flopped onto the floor, her tail knocking over the washing hamper as she fell. Cleo groaned. She was going to have to think of something else.

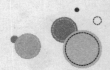

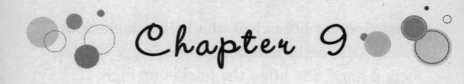

Chapter 9

Rikki was sitting by herself at the Juice-Net Café, idly turning the pages of a magazine. She was staring at the articles but she wasn't reading a single word. Emma and Cleo were the only friends she'd made since she'd moved to this new school and she'd fought with them already.

I've wrecked everything, she thought to herself, sadly. If only she had a bit more patience. Just like always, she opened her mouth and said whatever she was thinking. She felt really guilty about what she had said – she knew that she must have hurt their feelings. As always, now that her first flare of temper had passed, she could see that she had over-reacted. But she *was* sick of their whinging. They couldn't see the positives!

She felt a tap on her shoulder and looked up, staring straight ahead. She didn't want to see

anyone one right now, and her nerves bristled.

"Rikki, can I sit?" asked a nervous voice. It was Lewis.

"I certainly hope so," Rikki replied. "Just not with me."

Why can't he go and bother someone else? she thought. Lewis was the last person whose company she wanted.

Ignoring Rikki's sarcasm, Lewis slid into the seat opposite her and put his hat down on the table. Rikki stared at him in disbelief. Didn't this boy understand a 'get lost' comment when he heard one? She swiped her magazine to the floor with one flick of her hand and glared at him, her eyes burning into his like deadly lasers. It was very off-putting and Rikki knew it. That glare had got rid of a lot of unwanted company over the years.

Lewis looked at her face and swallowed a few times – he really didn't like her expression. *That's the kind of face that poisons a whole football team in half a second*, he thought. But

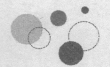

he had to speak to someone, and she was the only one around who could help. So he took a deep breath and started to speak. He had planned out exactly what he would say while he was plucking up the courage to come over, but he seemed to have forgotten some of the words.

"I know we've had our differences," he began, as Wilfred walked up and put a cola down in front of him. "Thanks ... um ... er ... but I want to know what's wrong with Cleo."

It made Lewis nervous just *talking* to Rikki. Now she was staring at him through half-closed eyes, as if she was listening to a particularly stupid slug trying to speak. She was silent for a long time, and he was just about to repeat the question when she shrugged her shoulders and opened her mouth.

"What makes you think there's anything wrong?" she snapped out, as if the act of speaking to him was a supreme effort.

Typical, thought Lewis. *You ask a question and you get a question in return*. He felt so

irritated that he forgot to be nervous.

"Well," he said, "I've asked her to go to Miriam's party, like, a *hundred* times and *every* time she changes her mind."

"*Maybe* … she doesn't like you," smiled Rikki, gasping and widening her eyes as if she had just had some sort of amazing revelation. "Did you think about that?"

"Yes, actually it did cross my mind," said Lewis, who was beginning to pick up on the sarcasm vibe. He acted looking depressed for a moment, and then perked up. "But then I thought, oh no, no, no, she hangs around with you so her standards must be pretty low."

Lewis smirked at her, mentally chalking one up to himself. *Maybe she'll talk to me if she respects my dazzling wit*, he thought.

Rikki rolled her eyes theatrically. "Goodbye, Lewis."

She waited for him to leave, but he didn't budge. He was staring at her in frustration.

Rikki was new, but suddenly she was as close to Emma and Cleo as if they had known each other all their lives. He didn't understand it, but he did know that if anyone could explain what was going on, it was Rikki.

"Look, can you tell me what's wrong or not?" Lewis begged.

"Not!" she snapped back, drumming her fingers on the table next to Lewis's cola. She just wanted to be left alone. Why was that so hard for him to understand?

"*Please*?" said Lewis. "I know there is!"

Rikki was really starting to get annoyed. *He never gives up!*

"Look, I'm not even speaking to her at the moment, okay?" she replied. "I'm just trying to be alone right now, so ... if you could just ... just ..."

Her hand clenched into a fist on the table. Even mentioning her argument with Cleo was making her feel upset, and she wasn't about to

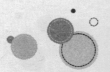

let Lewis McCartney see her weaker side. The very thought made her furious. Then she frowned as she realized that she could feel her anger channelling into her *hand*. It was the weirdest sensation – really tingly. It was almost like …

"What the–?" yelled Lewis, breaking into her thoughts.

His cola, which was on the table between them, was steaming and bubbling over like a witch's potion in a movie! He reached out and picked it up.

"Ow!" he shrieked, putting it down again and shaking his hand. "It's *hot*!"

Rikki stared at Lewis, then at the bubbling glass of cola, and finally down at her own hand. She clenched and unclenched it a few times, thinking hard. Then a real smile spread over her face.

"Is this somebody's idea of a joke?" Lewis muttered as he blew on his hand.

Rikki barely heard him. She forgot all about the stupid party and her argument with Emma and Cleo. She thought back to the day in Cleo's room when Emma and Cleo had shown what they could do with water. Cleo had made it rise out of a glass like a column. Emma had made it freeze with a flick of her hand. But Rikki hadn't been able to do a thing. She had thought that meant she didn't have a power like the other two. But what if she was wrong? What if she just hadn't been in the right frame of mind?

Rikki jumped up and left the Juice-Net Café while Lewis was arguing with Wilfred about his boiling cola. She raced down to the beach and over to the secluded place they had visited the day before. She couldn't wait to see if she was right. She had been really angry and Lewis's cola had boiled ... it couldn't just be a coincidence, could it?

Rikki walked up the beach between the rocks, looking for a place to test her theory. She

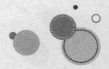

saw a small rock pool and looked all around, checking that no one was nearby. Then she bent down, holding out her hand above the small pool of water. Now that she had an inkling of what her power was, she didn't need to be angry to channel it. She could think of a better way than that!

Rikki let out a long breath and concentrated. She remembered how Emma had talked about exercising control, and she focused her mind on all the hottest things she could imagine – chillies, the sun, hot sand under her feet ...

Immediately the rock-pool began to boil, like water bubbling on the stove. Rikki glanced around again, checking that no one was coming. Then she clenched her fist over the water and it bubbled even more furiously. Steam rose from the water like smoke from a fire. Rikki kept going until all the water had evaporated from the pool. Then she stood up, threw back her head and laughed in sheer delight.

She had finally found her power – and it was *hot*!

Chapter 10

Later that day, Emma ran happily down the steps to the canal path, where Rikki was waiting for her. Now that she had given herself time to think, she had realized how ungrateful she and Cleo must have sounded the day before. She had decided to take a leaf out of Rikki's book and enjoy what she *had*, not moan about what she had lost. Now she just had to explain all that to Rikki.

"I'm glad you called," she said as soon as she saw her friend.

Rikki was leaning casually against the railings on the side of the canal. She beamed when she saw Emma.

"I'm sorry I was talking about all that negative stuff before," Emma continued. "I'm not normally like that, it's just…"

"Em, it's cool," said Rikki, the big smile still

plastered over her face.

Rikki had called Emma as soon as she had left the beach. It had been really hard not to blurt out her news over the phone, but Emma had to *see* this! She had tried to get hold of Cleo too, but for some reason she wasn't answering her phone.

Emma relaxed, realizing that Rikki wasn't the sort of person to need long explanations or heartfelt apologies. She and Cleo had really got under Rikki's skin the day before, but that was all over now. It was great to see her back to her usual, laid-back self.

"I need to show you something," said Rikki, jerking her thumb over her shoulder and walking off. She couldn't wait to see the look on Emma's face.

Rikki led the way down to their secret spot on the beach, refusing to give Emma a single clue about what she was going to show her. They reached the water, exchanged a look and a

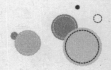

smile, and then waded in up to their waists. Ten seconds later they were diving through the softly lit blue underwater world that they were both coming to love. Each time they entered it they found new things to amaze and surprise them, and Rikki even forgot about her new power when she saw a school of fish coming towards her that were all the colours of the rainbow.

This is the best feeling in the world, Emma thought as she shot through the water like a golden flash. *If only Cleo could be here with us*. She was determined to get her friend into the water next time. Emma grinned as she watched Rikki tickling the fish and darting away. Okay, so she wasn't going to be able to enter swimming competitions any more. She was still able to swim – faster and further than ever before!

After about 15 minutes of playing with the fish and spinning through the water, Rikki beckoned to Emma and headed back to the shore. They surfaced, laughing, and then pulled themselves

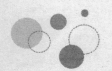

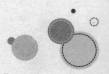

onto some rocks. It was an ideal place to dry off, overlooking the sea but hidden from the beach. The two girls lay next to each other, giggling and waiting for the sun to dry them off.

"Okay, I'm officially curious," Emma admitted at last. "What do you want to show me?"

Before Rikki could open her mouth to answer, they heard Lewis's voice behind them.

"Is that you guys?" he demanded. "Are you naked again?"

Rikki and Emma looked at each other in horror. They hadn't heard Lewis coming over the sand, but he was carrying his fishing gear and he obviously intended to stay there for a while. He had heard their voices and could just see the tops of their heads over the rock. They ducked down and he rose up on his tiptoes.

Rikki looked at Emma, searching for inspiration. What excuse did they have this time?

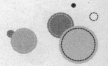

"Um ... we're having a bit of a girl talk, Lewis," she said eventually.

"Yes, but are you *naked*?" asked Lewis again.

"*Go*, Lewis!" said Emma, desperately.

If he came any closer he'd see them!

"No, no, I'm here to fish," said Lewis, getting annoyed. He couldn't allow these girls to take over his secret hideout – naked or not. "I'm having withdrawals, I need the relaxation. If anyone's going, it's you guys."

"Don't push it, Lewis," Rikki warned him.

"Yeah, shouldn't you be following Cleo around?" snapped Emma.

If she thought that would get rid of him, she was wrong. Rikki hadn't had a chance to tell her about Lewis's worries, and the mention of Cleo's name just opened up a whole new can of worms.

"*No!*" Lewis exclaimed loudly. "No way! I'm totally over that, trust me. I don't know what's going on with Cleo lately, she just can't make up

her mind."

As Emma stared at him in surprise, Lewis's phone beeped; he had a new text. He pulled the phone out of his back pocket and squinted at it in the sun. Then his expression darkened and he scowled.

"You see what I mean?" he said, wondering if he would ever understand women. "It's Cleo. She's going to the party … *again*. I give up."

Horrified, Emma turned to Rikki. How could Cleo be going to the party? They had to do something quickly! But there was no way they could move right now. Emma turned back to Lewis in a panic.

"Lewis, you've got to do us a favour," she declared. "Make sure Cleo doesn't go to the party on her own. Call her back."

"No, I'm here to fish," said Lewis, shaking his head.

He was sick of being bossed around by everyone – especially these two girls. Cleo could

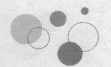
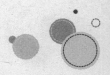

go to the party by herself and smile at surfing champs all day long for all he cared. He ground his teeth.

"Lewis, this is important," Rikki chimed in, fixing him with a fierce blue gaze. "She could be in trouble."

"I'm not some lackey," huffed Lewis as he got out his phone and hit a button to dial the sender of the last message. "I'm not some all-purpose servant." He held the phone up to his ear. "You really think you can tell me what to do and I'll jump?" He listened to his phone for a moment and then brought it away from his ear. "Her phone's off."

Emma felt sick with worry for her friend. Why hadn't she called Cleo that morning? *I might have known that she would still be thinking about Miriam's party*, Emma told herself. *But I was too busy worrying about my swimming training and that stupid argument with Rikki, and now look what's happened.*

"She could be in *big trouble*, Lewis," Rikki

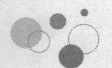
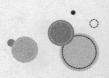

said. "You like her, don't you?"

"Well … in a friendship kind of way …" said Lewis, leaning shyly against his fishing rod. Why did girls always have to ask such embarrassing questions?

"Well?" asked Rikki again.

Lewis pulled a face, but he already knew the answer. He picked up his fishing gear and hurried back up the beach. He would never forgive himself if anything happened to Cleo.

Emma and Rikki looked at each other as Lewis left. They had to get dry and get over to Miriam's as fast as they could.

As they waited in the sun, Rikki told Emma about the power she had discovered. Emma was amazed, and they immediately both had the same idea.

If we were dry, we'd get our legs back and we could get going, Rikki thought. *This is the perfect chance to use my power! But …*

Emma made the suggestion, but Rikki shook

her head. She was too scared of burning them both – she didn't really know how to control her power, and she was so worried about Cleo that she didn't think she could focus her mind enough. She remembered the boiling cola and the rock pool she had evaporated. It was just too much of a risk. Cleo might not even be in trouble – and Lewis was already on his way.

Emma was frustrated, but she completely understood. She had been practising with her power for days now, and she was still a little freaked out by it. Besides, they were almost dry. As soon as the sun evaporated the last drops of water from their bodies, there was a rush of blue light and they had their legs back.

There was no time to lose! They scrambled to their feet and raced up the beach after Lewis, hoping that they would be in time.

I've got a really bad feeling about this, thought Rikki.

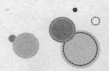

Chapter 11

It had taken Cleo ages to decide what to wear to the party. It had to be something that would protect her from any stray drops of water – something that would make her feel safe. She had taken so long to choose her outfit that she was worried the party would be over already. But when she walked up Miriam's front path, she could hear the unmistakeable sounds of laughter and music.

I hope I can pull this off, thought Cleo as she knocked on the front door. *I guess Emma and Rikki don't care about parties, but I want to be able to have some fun – even if I am a fishy freak!*

The door was immediately flung open and Miriam and Tiffany stood in front of her. They looked disappointed to see it was only Cleo, but their disappointment soon turned to amazement when they saw what Cleo was wearing.

Cleo held Miriam's gaze with a huge smile, trying to look as if it was completely normal to turn up for a pool party wearing a winter coat, a woollen scarf and thick gloves.

"Hey, it's a pool party, remember?" said Miriam, raising her eyebrows as she looked Cleo up and down.

"I remembered," replied Cleo. "It's just that I've got this terrible cold, so I won't be swimming. *At all*. So where's Byron?"

Cleo peered past Miriam into the house, trying to catch a glimpsing of the surfing hero.

Miriam looked at Tiffany.

"I'm sure he'll be here any minute," she said.

Tiffany nodded – she always agreed with anything Miriam said.

Cleo grinned. She hadn't missed Byron then!

"You're really keeping that on?" said Miriam, pointing to Cleo's outfit.

"Oh yeah," said Cleo, smiling. "You can't be too careful with a cold."

She suddenly realized that she didn't *sound* very much as if she was nursing a cold. She pulled out a tissue and blew her nose dramatically. Miriam and Tiffany looked at each other in disgust.

"Eww," said Tiffany. "Gross!"

"Cleo, I don't think it's a good idea that you're here," said Miriam, her eyes cold. "Sick people make me feel ... *sick*."

"You should go," said Tiffany, laughing slightly. She couldn't quite believe that this super-uncool girl thought she would fit in at Miriam's super-cool party.

"*No* ... I'm fine," said Cleo with desperation in her voice. "Really, it's *nothing* — I can still party!"

Miriam looked doubtfully at Cleo. She didn't want to let her in. On the other hand, she didn't want to stay this close to her, and at least there was no way that Cleo was going to outshine her.

"*Whatever*," she said eventually, stepping

aside to let Cleo in. "Just go outside and ... don't touch anything."

"Okay," said Cleo as she stepped into the hallway.

"And ... don't try any drinks," said Miriam.

"Fine," said Cleo.

"Better yet, just ... stay away from everybody," said Miriam finally, in a last-ditch attempt to get rid of Cleo.

"You got it!" said Cleo with a big smile. She was just happy to get in the door!

As Cleo walked past them and out to the back garden, Miriam exchanged a spiteful glance with Tiffany.

"Loser," she snapped.

Tiffany nodded in agreement as Miriam swung the door shut.

Cleo walked out to the pool, looking around at all the guests. Miriam's house backed onto the

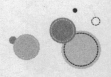

canal, and it was a wonderful venue for a party. All the girls were wearing fantastic pool-party outfits – one girl was wearing a leopard-print tankini that Cleo would have loved. *Some chance*, she thought bitterly. *I'll never be able to wear a bikini again!*

Whatever Miriam's failings as a friend, there was no denying that she could throw a fabulous party. There were huge balloon trees in pots all around the poolside. There was an enormous table spread with delicious-looking food and brightly coloured fruit-juice cocktails. Candy-coloured inflatables were floating on the water.

Cleo paused and stared at all the laughing, smiling guests. Everyone seemed to be having so much fun. Her heart sank as she realized what a mistake she had made. She should never have come. She was just going to spend the whole time feeling like an outsider.

The kids who were hanging around the drinks table turned to see the new arrival. Cleo's heart sank even further as she realized who they

were. *Oh no!* she groaned inwardly. *It's Zane and Nate and their stupid mates!* A bad situation had just got a lot worse.

Cleo turned to go back, but she was too late. They had already spotted her, and this time there was no one around to protect her.

"Look who's here," Zane said as he walked towards her, wearing a nasty grin. "Just when we wanted a bit of fun."

"No, get back," said Cleo.

She suddenly felt really frightened. Zane was still furious with her, and this time he had all his friends with him.

"Don't be like that, Cleo," said Zane, still wearing that stupid grin. "You had a good laugh when I got soaked last week." He was only a few steps away from where Cleo stood. "Now it's *your* turn."

He glanced at the pool and Cleo felt her heart hammering. She backed away from him, wishing that she had never come to Miriam's

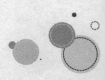

stupid party. If only she had listened to Rikki and Emma!

"I have a cold," said Cleo, holding up her tissue as if it would explain everything. "I can't go in the water. It's the flu actually ... and it's catching."

She was stammering now, hoping for some sort of miracle. She couldn't go in the water! Her secret would be out, and her life would be over!

Zane and his friends came closer. Behind her, two others blocked her exit. There was only the canal on one side and the pool on the other. *There's no escape!* Cleo thought in terror.

"Come on, it's swim time," Zane said. "You're going in."

"It could even be pneumonia," said Cleo, staring around wildly at the faces that surrounded her. She could feel her head swimming and her palms were sweating with fear.

"Cleo … Cleo … Cleo," he chanted.

Zane was not prepared to listen to anything she had to say. He wanted his own back, and he was determined to get it. No sad, whining little loser like Cleo Sertori was going to make a fool out of him and get away with it! He enjoyed the feeling of power it gave him to frighten someone else … and by now, Cleo was definitely frightened.

His friends joined in with the chant as they edged Cleo closer and closer to the pool.

"Cleo! Cleo! Cleo!"

Cleo was shaking now. She was almost at the edge of the pool – and there was nowhere to run to. Zane and Nate reached out their hands to grab her and she gave a little scream. She felt sick and dizzy. Even if she hadn't been a mermaid, she would have been petrified. But now her whole life could be ruined!

As the boys lifted her into the air, she pleaded with them to stop. There was no one to help her this time!

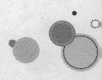

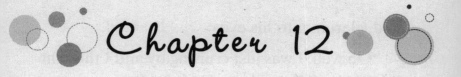

Chapter 12

Lewis dashed into Miriam's house, barged past groups of surprised guests and pelted out through the back door, still clutching his fishing equipment. He had raced to the house all the way from the beach, wondering what Emma and Rikki had meant when they said that Cleo could be in big trouble. He was just round the corner from the pool when he heard a loud voice ringing in his ears.

"*Lewis?*" snarled the voice, ending in a hiss.

Lewis stopped in his tracks and then turned on the spot, panting slightly. Miriam was walking slowly towards him, wearing a frosty expression. Her friend Tiffany was behind her, looking equally annoyed.

"I didn't think you were coming," Miriam

said, glaring into his eyes.

"Oh well, I was just cruising by and I thought I'd drop in," he said, avoiding her gaze.

"What's with the fishing gear?" asked Miriam in disbelief.

"I … er … never leave home without it," Lewis answered.

Bizarrely, this explanation seemed to be enough for Miriam. Lewis turned to go and then had a thought and whirled around to face Miriam again.

"Ah, have you seen Cleo?" he asked.

Miriam pouted, reminded of her other unwelcome guest. She looked Lewis up and down, taking in every detail of his non-designer sandals, his hopelessly outdated shorts and his old-man shirt. Her eyes came to rest on his bucket hat, and her pout turned into a sneer.

"She's round by the pool … spreading disease," she said eventually.

Lewis hurried towards the pool as Miriam

turned to Tiffany and rolled her eyes. She was starting to get really irritated. She had thrown this party for Byron, but he hadn't even turned up yet. Now these losers were turning her party into a complete disaster. When Byron finally arrived, she thought, he'd take one look at Cleo in her winter woollies and Lewis with his fishing gear, and run in the opposite direction!

At the poolside, Zane and Nate had picked Cleo up and were about to throw her into the pool. Nate was holding her legs and Zane was clutching her under her arms. They were swinging her backwards and forwards, laughing as she screamed. Behind them, several girls and boys were watching the entertainment and giggling. No one seemed to realize that Cleo was genuinely petrified.

"No! Please stop!" Cleo begged, struggling to escape. "Wait!"

"What do you reckon, Nate?" asked Zane, feeling a rush of adrenalin race through his body

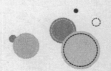

as his captive fought to get free.

"On three?" Nate suggested, his face pink and grinning.

A third boy came between them and for a wild moment Cleo thought that he was going to help her. But then he just smirked and put his hands under her back, helping Nate and Zane to hold her.

"One ... two ..." they counted aloud, swinging her out over the water.

This can't be happening to me! Cleo thought desperately. *This is like one of my worst nightmares! I'm going to turn into a fish in front of everyone from school and there's nothing I can do about it!*

"No!" she screamed again. "Please stop!"

Lewis rounded the corner just in time to see what was going on. He was horrified, knowing how scared Cleo was of the water – not to mention the fact that she couldn't even swim!

"Let her go, Zane!" he yelled.

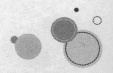

Cleo looked up, hope springing into her eyes. But Lewis was on the other side of the pool – there was no way he could reach her in time, and Zane knew it.

"If you insist," said Zane.

With one final swing they let go and threw Cleo into the water!

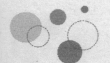
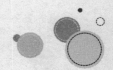

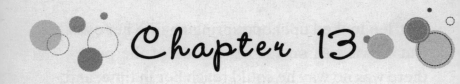

Chapter 13

For Cleo, it felt as if time slowed down and everything went into slow motion. She flew through the air and then began to fall. There was an almighty splash as she hit the water and sank directly to the bottom of the pool. Her thick winter clothes grew heavy with water, dragging her down. She couldn't see or hear anything, and blinding bubbles surrounded her. She was choking on the chlorinated water of the pool.

Cleo thrashed her arms and legs about wildly, trying to get some control, but for a moment she couldn't even tell which way was up. She could feel her hands and feet bumping against the hard tiles, but she didn't know whether it was the bottom or the sides. She didn't dare to open her eyes and she was too scared to stay still.

Above her, Zane and his friends were roaring

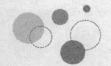

with laughter. She could hear their voices, weirdly distorted through the water.

"Do you even *have* a brain?" Lewis yelled at Zane, dashing over to where he was standing at the poolside.

"You told me to let her go …" said Zane. "I let her go!"

Zane's friends sniggered as he smirked and swaggered. Lewis just glared at him, itching to wipe that stupid smile off his face.

"Let's go and have a drink, boys," said Zane, pushing past Lewis and heading into the house. "Come on, everyone!"

Cleo had finally managed to swim up to the surface. She splashed across to the side and clung on as tight as she could, her waterlogged clothes weighing her down. Lewis rushed over to her and knelt down beside the pool as all the other guests followed Zane into the house.

"I'm so sorry about this," Lewis said.

He felt as if it was his entire fault. If only he

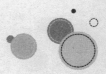

had run faster! If only he had thought of some way to stop Zane! Right now he wished he were as cool and popular as Byron. Byron would never have allowed Zane to throw his friend into the pool like that.

"Lewis, there's something you should know," said Cleo. She spoke rapidly, her voice shaking as she looked at her watch. There wasn't much time before things started to happen!

"No, no, you don't have to say anything," said Lewis. He hated hearing Cleo sound so upset. Whatever had been going on with her earlier that day, it was all forgotten now. He just wanted to help her and take that look of fear out of her eyes.

"No, I really do!" she told him firmly.

Cleo wasn't frightened of Zane and the other bullies any more. They had done their worst and she just had to deal with it. She was only frightened of what Lewis would say when he saw what she really was. She looked up at him as he knelt beside her and a sick feeling of dread

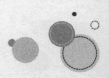

spread through her. How could she possibly make him understand? She didn't even understand it herself.

The water bubbled around her and her legs began to tingle. There were only a few seconds left! Lewis frowned and stared as the water roared and gurgled. *Has Miriam got some sort of spa pool?* he wondered.

"You know how I've been acting strange?" Cleo babbled as fast as she could. "Don't freak out, but–"

It was too late. The water stopped fizzing and bubbling, and finally cleared to reveal something long and golden ... something scaly and moving ... and totally unbelievable. Lewis stared in horror and amazement at Cleo's *tail*.

Cleo looked down at her tail and then back up at her oldest friend. She was still clinging to the poolside, hating the feeling of the water all around her. *He has to snap out of this!* she thought in desperation. *I have to get out of this*

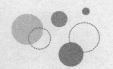

pool, and he's the only one who can help me!

Lewis opened and closed his mouth a few times, like a fish. He couldn't be seeing what he was seeing. It was completely impossible. He blinked a few times, wondering if he had got something in his eyes. *Yeah right*, he thought. *Something in my eyes that makes it look as if Cleo's got a tail.* He felt paralysed with shock.

"Lewis, you *have* to help me," pleaded Cleo.

Her voice acted like a release and Lewis finally regained some movement in his limbs. He stumbled backwards, away from the pool. His eyes were wide and unblinking, and he seemed to be unable to speak.

"Don't leave me!" Cleo begged. "I really need your help!"

Cleo stretched out her hand to him over the paving of the poolside. Lewis jerked his foot out of her reach and shook his head, biting his lip. Was he mad? Was he dreaming? This couldn't be real, right? He felt as if his chest was tightening up, stopping him from breathing or

speaking – even from thinking.

"Lewis – please!" Cleo said, still holding out her hand.

Her heart was thumping. Was Lewis going to abandon her now – just when she needed him most? She knew that she had sometimes taken him for granted before, but she couldn't believe that he would walk away when she was in so much trouble.

Lewis stared down at her and looked into her eyes. They were still Cleo's eyes – just the same. Warm and brown, with little flecks of green. Whatever else had happened, he could see that it was just the same person behind them, and she was scared.

He felt the tightness in his chest lessen and disappear. He stood up and his forehead creased into a frown. He paused for a moment, trying to take in what he was seeing. Then he reached down and clasped Cleo's hand in his.

Her face broke into a smile when she felt his warm, strong hand around hers. Now that she

had Lewis on her side, she suddenly felt as if everything was going to be all right.

Chapter 14

Suddenly, Cleo and Lewis heard the side gate open and Emma and Rikki charged in. Emma stopped abruptly when she saw Cleo in the pool and Rikki slammed into the back of her. They took in the scene and then stared at Lewis with their mouths wide open. They were too late!

"Where *is* everyone?" asked Rikki, horrified. *It's bad enough that Lewis knows*, she thought. *We can't let Miriam and her stupid friends see this too!*

"Er, they're inside," said Lewis as he tried to pull Cleo out of the pool. She was a lot heavier than she looked!

While Lewis struggled with Cleo, Emma raced around to the sliding back door, closely followed by Rikki. The door was closed, and inside they could see Zane and Miriam laughing with Nate and Tiffany. They weren't looking

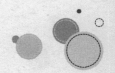

towards the door. Without even thinking, Emma raised her hand and used her power to freeze the lock, trapping all the guests inside. No one noticed – they were all too busy laughing about what Zane had done to Cleo.

At least that should keep them busy for a while, Emma thought. She looked at Rikki, who nodded her approval – they didn't need the rest of the school to know they were freaks of nature!

The two girls turned and ran back to the poolside. Lewis was still trying to pull Cleo out of the pool. Her tail was heavy, and it was hard for him to get a good grip on her wet hands. Without legs, Cleo couldn't do anything to help. He looked up as Emma and Rikki appeared at his side.

"Can you guys give me a hand?" he cried. "She weighs a ton!"

Cleo looked up at her friends apprehensively. *What have I done?* she thought in despair. *Not only have I given away my secret to Lewis, now*

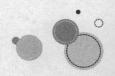

they're going to have to tell him about them as well!

Emma and Rikki didn't move, and Lewis turned to stare at them.

"We can't," said Emma, realizing that they were just going to have to tell him the truth.

Lewis looked at them uncomprehendingly and Rikki looked around as if searching for a solution to the mess. But she knew that there was nothing else for it. Lewis had to be told.

"If we get wet, we'll grow tails too," she said in a low voice. "Is that what you want?"

Lewis looked even more stunned, if that was possible.

"B-both of you?" he stammered eventually. He looked at Emma and Rikki in amazement, and then back down at Cleo. "*All* of you? *Seriously*?"

Cleo nodded sadly and Lewis took a deep breath. He couldn't think about this right now – he just had to get Cleo out of the water. With

one colossal heave he hauled her out of the pool and fell backwards, puffing and panting.

"I should've joined the gym," he said weakly.

No one laughed.

In the house, Zane had decided that he needed some air. He went to open the door, but it wouldn't budge.

"Who's locked the door?" he demanded.

"It's not locked," said Miriam with irritation in her voice.

She stood up and walked over to the door. *If you want something done properly*, she thought, *you have to do it yourself.*

She curled her hand around the door handle and tugged gently, hoping to make Zane look really stupid. But it wouldn't move. She pulled harder, resting her other hand against the glass to get a better grip. Still the door wouldn't open. Her friends gathered around her, staring as she wrestled with the door. What was going on?

Cleo lay on the poolside and flapped her tail forlornly. Lewis and Rikki looked down at her as Emma kept watch on the door.

"What are we going to *do*?" Cleo whined.

Rikki looked down at Cleo. She knew that she had to dry her out, but she didn't want to accidentally serve up fried fish! However, there was no time to waste in being afraid. This was an emergency.

"Get back, Lewis," said Rikki.

Lewis scrambled back as Rikki squatted down beside Cleo.

Oh well, here goes! she thought, taking a deep breath.

She held her hand a few inches above Cleo's body and forced her mind to remain calm. Then she thought of *warm* things – spa pools, medium curries and 22-degree days.

Lewis and Cleo looked at her in confusion. But then Cleo's expression turned to one of alarm as steam began to rise from her tail. There

was a hot, hissing sound as Rikki moved her hand slowly down Cleo's body.

"Ow, that stings," cried Cleo.

Rikki's heart jumped and she hurriedly thought of lukewarm tea, freshly baked cakes and summer evenings. The heat lessened slightly. She kept moving her hand up and down Cleo's body and the steam kept rising, until at last there was a blue shimmer and Cleo's tail had disappeared. She was wearing her wintry outfit once again.

"There you go, steam dried," said Rikki, smiling happily at Cleo, their argument completely forgotten.

Cleo sat up and wiggled her toes with relief.

"You found your power!" she said in delight, smiling back at Rikki.

Rikki just beamed at her. Lewis got to his feet and walked over to them. All this was happening much too fast for him – whatever 'all this' *was*.

110

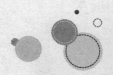

"Guys, *what* is going on?" he demanded.

Emma raced up to them and helped Cleo to her feet. She had been watching everything, and she knew that her iced-up lock wouldn't hold Miriam and her friends for very much longer.

"We'll explain later, Lewis," she said, pushing them all towards the side gate. They had to leave — right now!

Emma, Lewis and Cleo sped quickly out of the gate, but Rikki stopped and turned around. She looked at the party balloons and the colourful drinks, and she clenched her teeth together. It was obvious that someone had thought it would be a huge joke to throw Cleo into the pool, and Rikki hated bullies like that.

These people need to be taught a lesson! she thought.

Emma raced back through the gate and grabbed her by the arm.

"Rikki, come on!" she insisted.

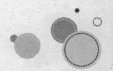

Emma ran out again, but Rikki didn't follow her. A mischievous smile illuminated her face. It was exactly the same smile she had worn when she took Zane's spark plug the week before. *And look how well that turned out*, she told herself. If it hadn't been for that spark plug, she would never have met Emma and Cleo, they wouldn't have been stranded on Mako Island and been turned into mermaids, and they would never have had all this fun!

Emma and Cleo would not have approved. But Emma and Cleo were not there.

Rikki raised her hand over the pool and slowly curled her fingers inward into a fist. She thought of the hottest thing she could imagine – the surface of the sun!

The effect was instantaneous. The pool began to boil and steam poured off it into the air. "I never liked pool parties anyway," laughed Rikki, lowering her hand. She took a final look at her handiwork and then ran out of the gate, just as Miriam finally got the back door open

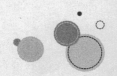

and rushed outside.

Miriam and her guests stared at the pool in disbelief. There was not a single drop of water left in it. The inflatables lay on the blue tiles and steam filled the air around them.

"What is going *on*?" squealed Miriam.

"You should *really* check your heating system," said Zane.

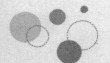
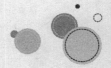

Chapter 15

Emma, Cleo, Lewis and Rikki raced away from Miriam's house and hurried along the grassy strip beside the beach. They were heading towards their secret place among the rock pools. They didn't say a word to each other, somehow knowing that they had to wait until they were completely alone before they could talk about what had just happened.

As they passed a group of trees, they saw Byron heading down to the water with his surfboard under his arm.

"Hey Byron!" yelled Lewis, stopping and grinning.

"Oh, hey guys," Byron said.

The girls paused and turned as Byron jogged over to them.

"Why aren't you at the party?" asked Cleo in astonishment.

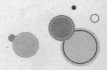

"Huh?" he asked, looking completely bewildered.

"The pool party?" Cleo reminded him. "The one Miriam's putting on for you?"

She couldn't believe he didn't remember a party in his honour!

"Miriam? She's the blonde one, right?" Byron asked, who was still a little confused. Now he thought about it, Miriam *had* mentioned a party to him, but she hadn't said anything about it being in his honour.

Emma grinned at Rikki as Cleo nodded. Miriam would be furious if she ever found out that Byron didn't even know who she *was*!

"Parties aren't really my thing," Byron added shyly. "See you, guys."

He smiled at them, waved his hand and ran down to the surf.

Emma watched him thoughtfully. He looked so free, racing towards the waves in the late afternoon sun. He looked much happier than all

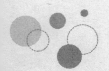

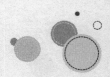

those spiteful kids who were waiting for him at Miriam's party.

"Nice board," said Emma, as she looked at Byron's professional surfboard.

"Nice pecs," said Cleo dreamily.

"Nice attitude," said Rikki, smiling.

They walked on, but Lewis stood still, gawping after Byron for a moment. Then he turned and ran to catch up with the girls.

When they reached their secret place, Cleo and Lewis perched on some rocks and Emma and Rikki sat opposite them. Rikki and Cleo looked expectantly at Emma, who sighed. *I guess I'm the designated speaker then?* she thought.

Lewis listened eagerly as Emma began to explain what had happened to them. With Rikki and Cleo butting in every now and then to add to her descriptions, she told him about how they had ended up drifting out to sea in Zane's boat; how they had paddled to Mako Island and

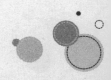

started climbing to try to get a phone signal. She explained how Cleo had fallen down a tunnel and they had followed her, eventually discovering the mysterious cave deep underground. Lewis listened in astonishment when she told him how the moon had shone down through the hole in the roof of the cave, and how the water around them had bubbled and glowed as if it was magic. Finally, she described how they had each discovered that they were mermaids, and that they had such incredible powers.

When she had finished, there was a moment of amazed silence. Of course, Rikki was the first to break it.

"This probably goes without saying, but if you tell, we maim you," she said.

"I'm not that *stupid*," said Lewis, annoyed. "If anyone found out, you'd end up as science experiments."

Rikki gave Cleo a meaningful look, and Cleo dropped her eyes. She finally realized just how

serious this was. She wished that she hadn't been so silly and gone to the pool party – except for the fact that Lewis knew about them now. Whatever Rikki said, Cleo knew that it was a good thing to have Lewis on their side.

There was a long silence as each of them thought about the amazing – and scary – things that had happened to them in the past week.

Emma was feeling glad that Rikki had stopped her before she could get too negative. Everything in her life was going to be different from now on, and there were going to be endless new challenges to face. But Rikki had shown her that just because everything had to change, that didn't mean that it was going to get worse. It might even get better. *I need to be more like Byron*, Emma told herself, remembering the surfing champ's great attitude. *Just go with the flow, and don't let anyone or anything fluster me.*

Cleo was thinking about how close she had come to danger at the party. Zane and his friends were such a bunch of idiots. But it had

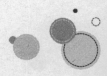

been her fault too, for not listening to her friends. She was determined to be more careful in future, and as far as she was concerned, being careful meant staying away from water. As she looked at Rikki and Emma, she knew that they were going to want to go back into the water – to continue the journey that had started on Mako Island. Cleo gave a little frown. She wasn't sure that she was going to be able to make that journey with them.

Now that the danger had passed, Rikki had forgotten all about it. She was revelling in the fact that she had finally found her power. *Just think of all the things I'll be able to do with this*, she thought in delight. *Hot drinks, instant heating – hey – I never need to be cold again!* Rikki didn't believe in regretting the past or wishing herself into the future. She believed in living for the present – and the present had never been so exciting!

Lewis's brain was ticking over at top speed. He was mentally listing all the books and

websites he was going to check out as soon as he got home. He couldn't wait to work out exactly how this had happened to the girls. He was sure that he could help – somehow. He looked at Cleo's worried face and smiled. Emma looked as serene as always, every hair in place. Even Rikki didn't look as scary as usual. Lewis watched them all and realized that for whatever reason this ... *thing* ... had happened to them, it had turned them into a team. Then he had a sudden realization. He was part of the team now too – and it felt good.

"I quit the swimming team today," said Emma.

"*Oh Emma*," said Cleo in her gentle voice. "I know how much that means to you."

She felt desperately sorry for her friend. It was as if all Emma's dreams were disappearing.

"Still ... what could I do?" said Emma, trying to smile ... and failing.

Rikki looked at her thoughtfully. She was just beginning to understand why Emma hadn't

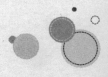

been full of excitement about becoming a mermaid. At first she had thought that Emma was way too uptight and obedient, but since then she had started to appreciate Emma's dedication and discipline.

"This whole thing is just out of control," said Cleo, waving her hands in the air. "It's just too big."

Lewis looked sideways at her and a small smile crinkled up one side of his mouth.

"Let me get this straight," he began. "You freeze things," he pointed at Emma. "You *explode* things," he smiled at Cleo, remembering the fire hydrant episode, which suddenly made perfect sense. "And you boil things," he said to Rikki. "And you all grow tails? It's just too bizarre!"

"Bizarre? Yep," said Emma. "Still ... sometimes it's good," she said, smiling at Rikki. "And sometimes it's ... not so good."

"It's ... it's ... it's ... I don't have a word for it," said Cleo, giving up.

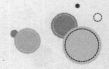

"I do," chimed in Rikki. "Three of them. Totally, absolutely, *awesome*!"

Emma and Lewis laughed, and Cleo put her chin on her hands. Rikki turned and gazed out to sea. Evening was drawing in and the waves were tipped with white. The late sun was sparkling on the water. Rikki smiled contentedly. Whatever was coming – whatever new dangers they were going to have to face, one thing was certain. Life was never going to be boring again!

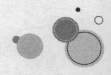